BEAUTY AND THE BEAST

A RETELLING BY H. Chuku Lee

ILLUSTRATIONS BY Pat Cummings

Amistad

An Imprint of HarperCollinsPublishers

To my family . . . past, present and future . . .   —H.C.L.

For Chris Cummings, my Beauty, and Chuku, my Beast   —P.C.

✦

With endless thanks to Barbara Lalicki for believing

Amistad is an imprint of HarperCollins Publishers.
Beauty and the Beast
Text copyright © 2014 by H. Chuku Lee
Illustrations copyright © 2014 by Pat Cummings
All rights reserved. Manufactured in China.
No part of this book may be used or reproduced in any manner whatsoever without written permission except in the case
of brief quotations embodied in critical articles and reviews. For information address HarperCollins Children's Books,
a division of HarperCollins Publishers, 195 Broadway, New York, NY 10007.
www.harpercollinschildrens.com

ISBN 978-0-688-14819-5

The artist used watercolor, gouache, pencil, and pastel on 300-lb. Fabriano Artistico hot-press paper
to create the illustrations for this book.
Typography by Martha Rago
18   SCP   10 9 8 7 6 5 4
❖
First Edition

◇ ◇ ◇ FIRST TOLD in 1740 by Madame Gabrielle-Suzanne Barbot Gallon de Villeneuve, *Beauty and the Beast* continues to capture the imagination of each new generation—authors, playwrights, filmmakers, and many, many others have been inspired by the tale.

Now we are delighted to share our vision with you. It is a fresh telling of an old story about love, magic, and the power of a promise.

We hope you profit from it.

FATHER had to hurry into the city on business, but before he rode off, my older sisters gave him a long list and asked him to buy them all sorts of finery.

Father asked what I wanted and I said, "A rose."

How could I know his promise to bring me a single rose would change all our lives forever?

When Father returned, he told us his trip had been a disaster. On the way home a storm had forced him off the road, and he found himself at the door of an enchanted palace. No one answered when he knocked, but invisible servants opened the door and gave him fresh dry clothes, a delicious meal, and a comfortable bed.

In the morning, as he was leaving, Father remembered his promise to me. He went to the enormous garden and picked a single rose. At that instant he heard an awful roar. Turning, he found himself face-to-face with a huge ugly Beast dressed in the latest fashion.

The Beast said that he loved his roses above all else and that Father would have to pay with his life for stealing one!

Falling to his knees, Father apologized and explained he was picking the rose for me, his youngest daughter, Beauty.

As Father wearily handed me the rose, he said, "I begged the Beast to let me live so I could see you, my family, one last time. The Beast paused, thought for a moment, and then made me promise to return to the palace for my punishment."

"Not alone!" I told Father. "I am going with you. It was, after all, my rose that caused this trouble."

As soon as we met, the Beast demanded to know if I would stay and live in his palace. At first I hesitated, but when the creature said he would spare Father's life if I did, I agreed to stay.

The Beast then promised me that I could have whatever I wanted—anything—except . . . I could not leave.

So saying, he let Father go.

Time passed. The Beast was very kind to me. His invisible servants gave me everything: my own rooms, good food, beautiful clothes, jewels, and even a magical mirror that let me see my family at home.

But . . . I could not leave!

I saw the Beast once a day at dinnertime. Gradually I realized that he was truly kind and would not hurt me. I began to look forward to his warm presence and friendly conversation each night.

Still . . . I could not leave!

One night, after an especially sumptuous meal, the Beast nervously asked me to marry him. I was so stunned, I heard myself saying no, without thinking.

The Beast roared loudly as if in pain, gazed at me sadly, and backed away.

After that, he often asked again.
And while I knew my feelings for
him were growing stronger, I
could not marry him.

Several months had passed when my magic mirror showed me that Father was ill. I told the Beast that I would die of sadness if I could not be with my father again. I promised him, saying, "Let me go home, and I will return to the palace in eight days."

The Beast opened a chest decorated with his family crest and handed me a gold ring studded with diamonds. "You only have to put it on your finger to go home, and again to come back."

Gazing at me, the Beast warned, "Remember your promise, or I, too, will die of sadness!"

I arrived home with a large trunk filled with beautiful clothes and jewels given to me by the Beast.

Father cried with surprise and almost fainted when he saw me.

Jealous of my fine clothes and jewels, my sisters were distant, but on the eighth day they begged me to break my promise to the Beast and stay longer.

"Never mind the Beast," they said. "You belong here with us."

I let myself be persuaded, unwilling to leave my father's side.

But on the tenth night I dreamed that the Beast was dying in the palace garden.

I couldn't stand the thought of hurting him and spent the rest of the night tossing and turning. In the morning, before anyone was awake, I put on my ring and returned to the palace.

I knew I had broken my promise. I thought that if
I changed into my most magnificent dress, I could
please the Beast and make it up to him.
I paced all day, waiting anxiously for dinnertime.
But the Beast did not appear.

In despair, I ran into the garden, where I found him moaning softly, lying near the pond. "I've killed my only friend!" Sobbing, I embraced his limp, ugly body.

Wait! There was a heartbeat!

Looking weakly up at me, the Beast said, "You have broken your promise! But I die content because I am able to see you one last time."

"Oh no you don't!" I cried. "You are going to live so we can be married! I realize now that I love you."

Then, amazingly, the Beast disappeared, and in his place stood a handsome prince. Smiling with gratitude and bowing, he told me that an evil fairy had cursed him to remain a Beast until a beautiful woman loved him for himself.

Father was the happiest I'd ever seen him as
the Beast and I exchanged rings at our wedding.
We all moved into the palace to spend the rest
of our days surrounded by roses.

Now . . . I would not leave!